Birds live in the air, dance in the air,
eat in the air.
They receive the sun's light before anyone else.
But they are born on the earth,
like you,
like me.

Para mis amigos,
hermanos del camino — RY

Published in 2021 by Groundwood Books / House of Anansi Press
groundwoodbooks.com

Groundwood Books respectfully acknowledges that the land on which we operate is the Traditional Territory of many Nations, including the Anishinabeg, the Wendat and the Haudenosaunee. It is also the Treaty Lands of the Mississaugas of the Credit.

We gratefully acknowledge the Government of Canada for its financial support of our publishing program.

With the participation of the Government of Canada
Avec la participation du gouvernement du Canada | Canadä

Library and Archives Canada Cataloguing in Publication
Title: Wounded falcons / words by Jairo Buitrago ; pictures by Rafael Yockteng ; translated by Elisa Amado.
Other titles: Halcones heridos. English
Names: Buitrago, Jairo, author. | Yockteng, Rafael, illustrator. | Amado, Elisa, translator.
Description: Translation of: Halcones heridos.
Identifiers: Canadiana (print) 20200402218 | Canadiana (ebook) 20200402234 | ISBN 9781773064567 (hardcover) | ISBN 9781773064574 (EPUB) | ISBN 9781773064581 (Kindle)
Subjects: LCGFT: Picture books.
Classification: LCC PZ7.B8857 Wo 2021 | DDC j863/.7—dc23

The illustrations were created digitally.
Design by Michael Solomon
Printed and bound in South Korea

WOUNDED FALCONS

Words by

JAIRO BUITRAGO

Pictures by

RAFAEL YOCKTENG

Translated by Elisa Amado

GROUNDWOOD BOOKS
HOUSE OF ANANSI PRESS
TORONTO / BERKELEY

The two of them are friends, and it was a bad day at school.
One black eye, a torn lip, fists clenched with rage.
Adrián gets into trouble with everyone.
Santiago never has any problems.
But the two of them are friends, and it was a bad day.

There they are, as always, in the same place,
   surrounded by weeds and garbage.
They are friends, and they sit in the middle of an
   empty lot that doesn't belong to anyone, where no
   one ever comes.
They light a fire against the cold. They prefer to be
   there together after school before going home.

Santiago sits in some clover and reads the books his
teacher lends him.
Adrián walks around, climbs trees, looks for little
creatures, and in the distance he can see the factory
where his mother works.

And in a clump of grass, he finds it.
A young wounded bird. Scared, unable to fly.
They look at each other with wide-open eyes.

Adrián uses his school jacket to wrap it up carefully.
He can feel its heat.
He can feel its strength and the beating of its heart.
"That's a kestrel, or a goshawk, or a sparrow hawk," says
    Santiago. "Someone hurt its wing with a stone."
"It's a falcon, and I'm going to take care of it," says Adrián.

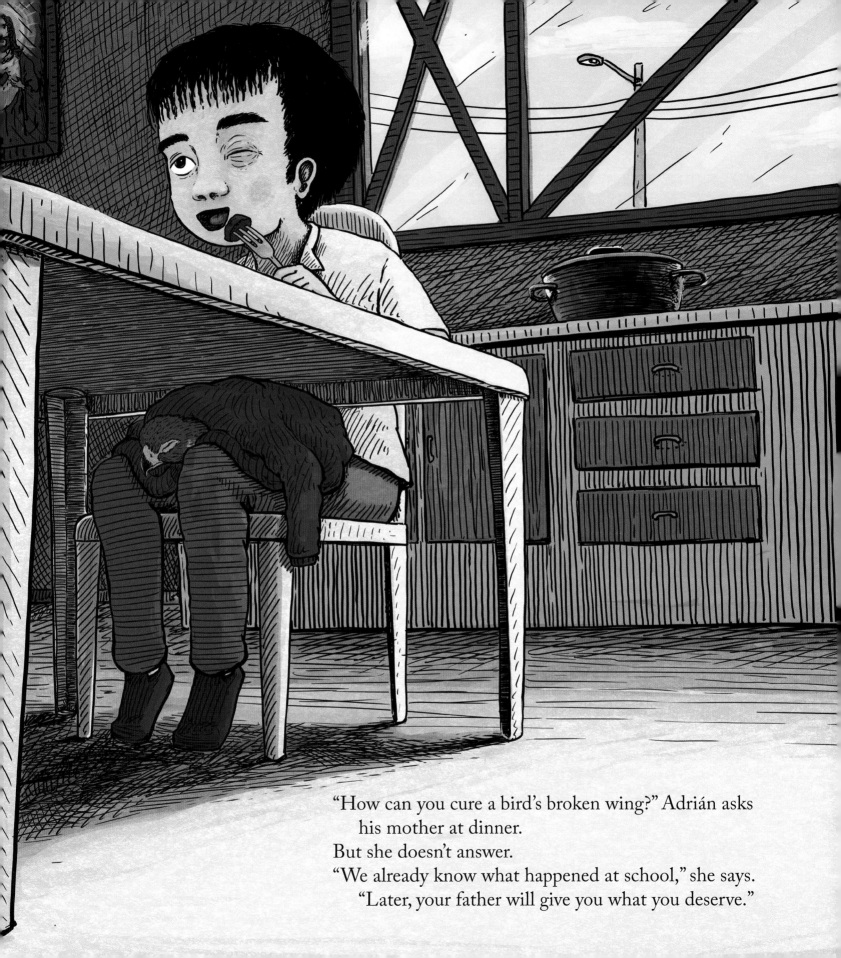

"How can you cure a bird's broken wing?" Adrián asks
his mother at dinner.
But she doesn't answer.
"We already know what happened at school," she says.
"Later, your father will give you what you deserve."

The next day the friends meet in the forgotten empty lot.
"You didn't come to school," says Santiago.
"I hid it in my house and then I came here with it. There
are street dogs and rats, and it can't protect itself."
"My uncle knows a guy who cures broken bones. A
broken wing is like a broken bone," explains Santiago.

The old guy who cures bones has never seen a falcon.
But he does his work carefully — checks the wing,
    straightens it, immobilizes it, bandages it. The falcon's
    head is in a small child's sock.
"It's scared, like me," thinks Adrián.

They hide a wooden box filled with straw high up in
a tree. That's where the falcon's house will be.
"The money to pay the old guy, where did you get it?"
asks Adrián.
"It was money I'd saved for Christmas."

For six weeks they take care of it. They feed it.
Until one day, when they remove the bandage,
    it can open its wings.
It is getting strong.

And in science class, even though the others laugh
and whisper, Adrián talks about birds of prey, about
their strength, about their beauty.
The teacher watches him. It's the first time he has
spoken in class.

When he is sad, Adrián climbs the tree and looks
at his friend, the falcon.
They know each other, they can feel their hearts
beating when they are together.

But one afternoon, when school gets
out, there is a violent rainstorm.
And they run.
They run to find the tree.

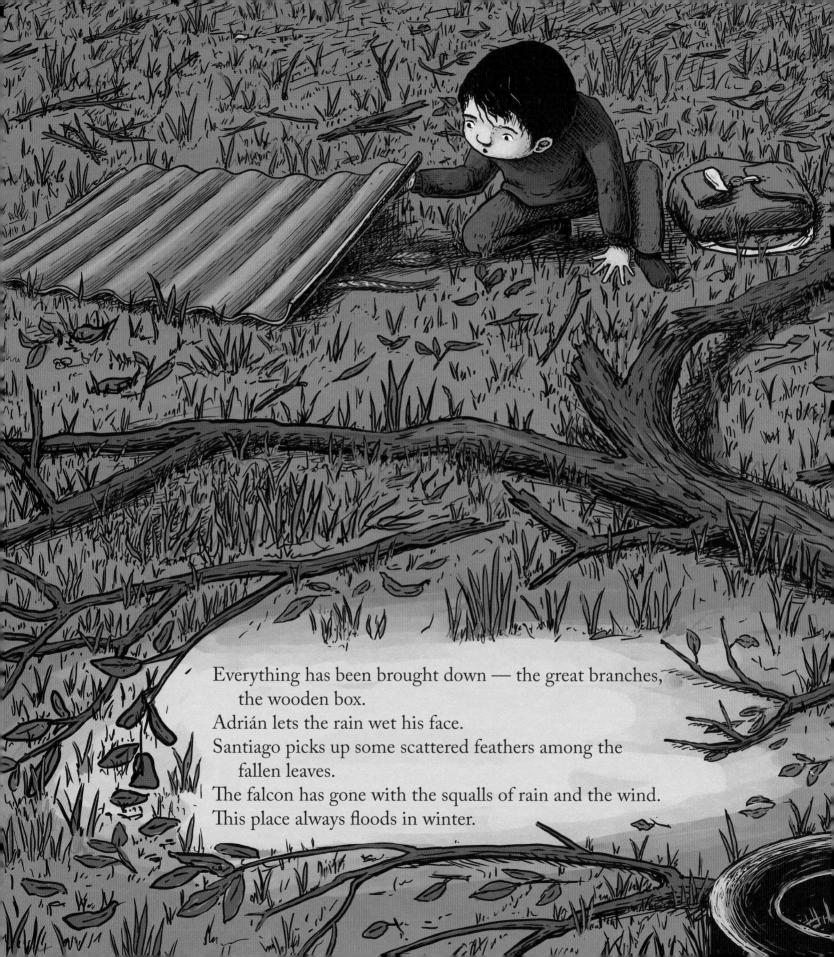

Everything has been brought down — the great branches, the wooden box.

Adrián lets the rain wet his face.

Santiago picks up some scattered feathers among the fallen leaves.

The falcon has gone with the squalls of rain and the wind.

This place always floods in winter.

The next day the friends go back to their lot, even though
    it's drizzling and it's cold.
And then all of a sudden, like a lightning bolt, a falcon
    dives from the sky and catches a pigeon.
And it screams from the top of the broken-down wall to
    salute them.

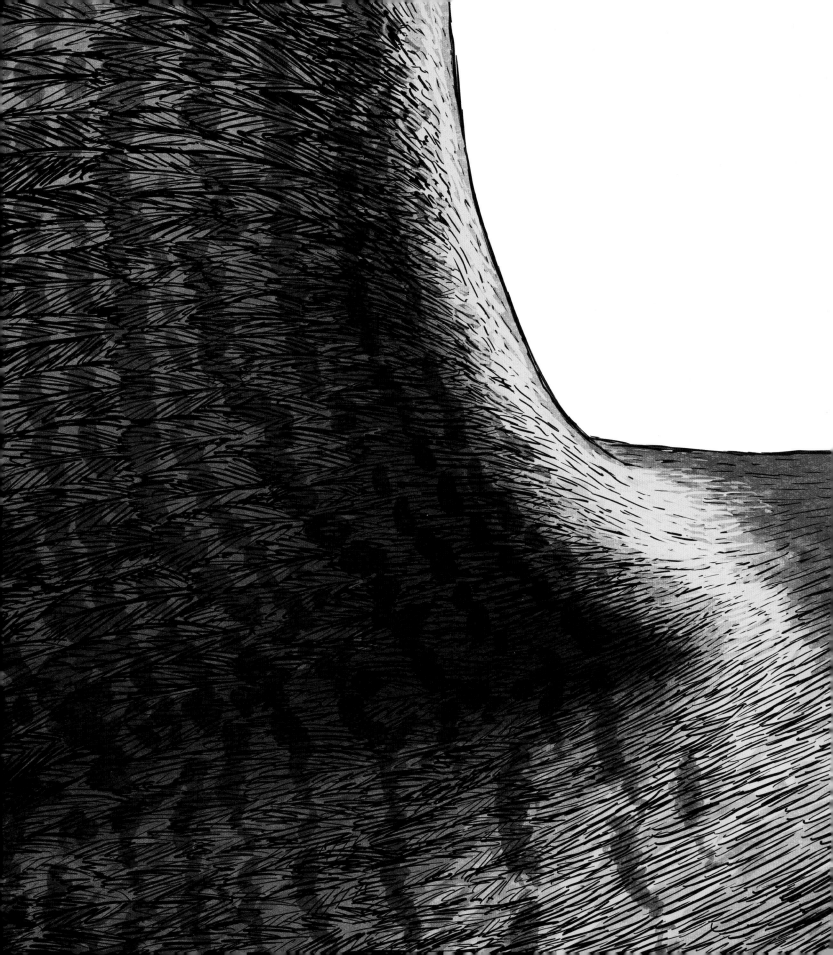

Is it the same one?
To Santiago it seems different — another bird. He isn't sure.
But he had never seen any other falcon in this neighborhood
    that has been forgotten by everybody.
And he sees tears on his friend's cheeks — his friend who
    never cries, not even when they were both little children.

They go home in silence, and Santiago thinks that
    Adrián has a big heart, even if he gets into trouble.
Tomorrow when they leave school to go to the empty
    lot that belongs to no one, where no one comes,
    maybe they can see the falcon hunting again, and
    they will be closer than ever.